Aidan Gregory is a self-taught writer. He enjoys creating stories by reading books about history, medicine, the sciences, various arts, spirituality of all kinds, occult topics, and many novels.

For my lovely Muses.

Aidan Gregory

MARTIAN CONCERNS
AND OTHER TALES

AUSTIN MACAULEY PUBLISHERS™

LONDON · CAMBRIDGE · NEW YORK · SHARJAH

A CIP catalogue record for this title is available from the British Library.

ISBN 9781035836420 (Paperback)
ISBN 9781035836437 (ePub e-book)

www.austinmacauley.com

First Published 2024
Austin Macauley Publishers Ltd®
1 Canada Square
Canary Wharf
London
E14 5AA

In 2013 a researcher found a Curiosity Rover picture in a NASA archive of what appeared to be a woman on the surface of Mars. The picture was dubbed 'Mars Woman.'

2072—Four travellers on a solo flight from Earth are about to arrive on Mars.

Freddy, a slim, gaunt faced man, was sitting at the back wall of his sleeping compartment.

"You were rolled up in a ball and sobbing. We sedated you." Fiona said.

"I wasn't sobbing," Frederick protested, "My nerves. We've been out here for 43 days and we have been tortured," Freddy's voice became shrill, "the ghosts are torturing us and you know it!"

Fred had gone berserk. Ghosts had appeared to him in his bunk one too many times, and he simply lost it. Terrified, he ran around the ship shouting obscenities.

The others left the small room. "We'll check in later Fredrick," said Frank on the way out. "Sleep meds worked on him. Worked for me a little," Frank said in a tired, cracking voice, "I'm numb from head to toe. Matter of fact, I think I'll try taking a nap again," as he tread lightly toward the lounge squinting even in the soft light of the long corridor. He squared his stocky frame, readied for battle and said, "I'm used to the torments". He knew he was lying.

"We need to talk about what we're going to do with Freddy," Deirdre said to the back of his head in an annoyed tone, "what to say about him at Mars base?"

"Later," he replied gruffly.

Fiona and Deirdre watched him until he walked around a corner.

Dierdre said, "I'll see if I can focus on 'them' and let him get some sleep. You want to sleep too?"

"Forget it. I'm going to get my things together", Fiona said,

"Seven hours and we'll be on the surface." They were as exhausted as Sam.

The ship was owned by partners Virgo Space and Space Xcel and was one of a fleet of twelve. The Colonising of Mars Phase I was a project by Galactic Industries and had been on the surface for ten years. There were managers, scientists, agriculturalists, technicians, construction workers, construction equipment/supplies, fully equipped labs, and living quarters, all in many very large geodesic domes and tunnels. Domes also housed small farms and recreation areas. Energy was supplied by a compact underground nuclear power plant.

The decision was made to build the facility in a narrow valley only a few kilometres from the Valles Marineris. The steep hills helped to shield against the wind and sandstorms.

Water was found deep in the canyon at 17.6 S 61.4W. A frozen reservoir—trillions of gallons. The water was processed to make it potable and nitrogen and oxygen were extracted.

Argon was transported from Earth then the air components were mixed and steadily released. There were many chemically cooled nuclear power plants all over Mars that powered a planet-wide array of electromagnetic antennas emitting a constant pulse to match that of Earth by a third.

Huge suction devices near the power plants drew in existing carbon dioxide from the atmosphere and split it into carbon monoxide and oxygen ions. The oxygen ions then combined with each other to produce oxygen gas. This additional oxygen would react with UV rays to create ozone in Mars' stratosphere.

The atmosphere would be ready to live outdoors in another five years. A population would be needed—Phase Two.

A while later Deirdre and Fiona were sitting in the spacious galley staring at the floor-to-ceiling mural of Mars that covered one wall. In the centre there was a live feed TV streaming Mars from a satellite. They watched it as the ship sailed steadily closer and sipped freeze-dried coffee with powdered cream. Fiona's red hair was dishevelled and frizzy. Her eyes were puffy, her skin pale. Deirdre looked the same though she kept her head shaved.

"I can't stand these rotten ghosts," Fiona whispered.

"I know, I know. But stay calm," Deirdre answered, her voice gruff.

She put her cup down and rubbed her darkly circled eyes.

About an hour before, Frank had reclined on a large comfortable couch. "Dim lights", he said and closed his eyes. He took a deep breath and sighed. He dreaded being jolted awake when he was almost asleep. He was determined not to crack like Freddy. He had upped his dosage of sleep medication, and it had been working but only for a few hours at a time. He drifted off.

The unseen torments started about three weeks before.

They were seeing glimpses of people—different-looking, like old photographs. Then the sleep disorders started. Loud noises near their ears or down the halls, even pinching and shocking sensations. It went on for a week before they started taking sleep meds. Some days were worse than others, but then Fredrick cracked.

About an hour into his snooze, a full-bodied dark-haired woman wearing a long tight dress with aqua, beige, red, and green stripes walked into the lounge. The attractive woman slowly laid on top of Frank, who happened to roll on his side. She lay there a moment, looking at him. With the red-painted nail of her forefinger, she played with a stray follicle sticking out of his nose. Her face was close to his.

He started twitching it and, after a minute, he woke up. At first the extra weight on him didn't register but then he opened his eyes and looked directly into the woman's burning coals.

As he jumped up in terror she disappeared and it took all of his wits to keep from screaming and tearing up and down like Freddy.

Frank stalked into the galley, his long black hair flying, face flushed, eyes hollow and wild.

He said, "I've had it. I'm getting the transport ready. As soon as we're in orbit I'm going down. The ground crew can come up for cargo; I don't care about a wasted trip," he explained what had happened, and Deirdre said, "Just awhile longer; let's keep each other awake."

Frank shrugged his shoulders and turned away. Deirdre shook her head and then shot a worried gaze at Fiona.

In his compartment, Fredrick was half asleep. He was visualising one of the summer vacations he and his family had taken at Lake George one August. They had brought their boat with them and motored out to an island campground. The children were young, seven and nine.

He remembered that the campsite was between a few tall oaks and surrounded by high pachysandra bushes. The kids hopped around playing some made-up game. His wife, Nadia, was standing nearby in the scattered sunlight, slightly tanned, her buttery blond hair glowing.

She was so happy. Her eyes gleamed but with a hint of anxiety. She worried about the children with all that water around. He began to weep and said out loud, "My wife—A Vision…."

"Good looking kids, too," someone said. Torn from his reverie, Freddy popped his eyes open.

Standing with his back against the door was an old man in rumpled clothing. He had a full head of grey hair and O-shaped eyeglasses on a face that was hard to describe except to say it was in folds from under his eyes to his double chin. His colleague, the attractive dark-haired woman, was standing next to him. Oddly, Freddy wasn't the least bit frightened any longer. He was half expecting to talk to one of the ghosts. A little extra sleep relaxed him. "Couldn't resist the redhead? Your wife throw you out?"

Freddy was stunned. How could he know that? He said, "Wait, you're both hallucinations. I've lost my mind, and I'm amazingly calm."

"You're not hallucinating. Yes, we are ghosts, Mars Intelligence. We live in a spirit realm around Mars, but we can appear in 3rd density where you live. It's harder to appear in the third density on Earth. Negative energy is everywhere. 'Welcome to outer space.' Freddy thought.

"Galactic Industries is beginning to populate our home. You and your crew are in Phase 2, correct?" Fred nodded.

"You'll operate the In Vitro Fertilisation Clinic, and you're a geneticist. And the others have gene editing experience."

Freddy's head shrunk into his shoulders. There were a few moments of silence.

"A bad rich guy gave you, Frank, Deirdre, and Fiona, large sums of cash and between the three of you forging reports and switching containers you were able to smuggle the samples from Earth. I know where they are. And what are those samples, Fred? You were going to come to my home and experiment and create what Fred?"

Freddy was stunned. After ruminating, he said, "We need to find more suitable, sturdy skeletal frames for the people to exist in space environments."

The old man had a terrible look on his face.

"OK, what exactly are you driving at?" Fred said, still surprised that he was talking to an apparition made manifest.

"I'm talking about me and my folks re-incarnating. You know what I'm talking about."

"Did I really know there would be Martians ready to reincarnate into test tube babies?" Fred replied sarcastically.

"And you're missing something," the old man went silent then continued, "obviously, a small detail to you. Those who bribed you want you to create a class structure their future families can control. An elite class of modern humans with enhanced DNA to handle the rigors of space and also a grunt class. What's this class of grunts Freddy?"

Freddy looked away but couldn't help betraying a nervous grin.

In a gruff tone the old man said, "Do you think we want to be Neanderthals or Cro-Mags?"

His colleague shot Freddy a nasty look.

"And what about ethics? The preliminary tests with Neanderthal DNA looked promising, to you, but now you need specimens and you know there will be many birth defects until you get it right. Oh yes, I read your notes. Deirdre has offered to bring one to full term. If you don't like the results you'll kill the newborn monstrosity and start again?"

Freddy wriggled a bit. His own kids came to mind but he immediately steeled himself and thought about all the problems in the world and how it was due to human emotions.

A class of elite intellectuals makes the rules and this would ultimately make for a more peaceful society especially if most of the emotive body chemical combinations could be curtailed for the masses. His mind was made up on that.

"It wouldn't take long in test tubes to see if an embryo can make it to full term. All great achievements are marred by failed attempts. And Neanderthal/Cro-Mag DNA tests are just experiments".

"Ah—yes."

The old man looked at Freddy with piercing eyes.

For a split second, Freddy caught a glimpse of something very dark pass behind them.

Then he said, "I'll be back in a while. I'm assuming you'll destroy the samples." Freddy blinked his eyes; the old man and woman were gone.

The ship was in orbit and almost above Mars Base. Frank notified them that they were on their way down. Gathering his things, Frank said, "I'm taking only what I need for now."

"What do we do with Freddy? We can't leave him here," Fiona said.

"Let's check. If he seems ok we'll let him out", Frank replied. They left their things in the first transport and went to Freddy. Frank removed the socket wrench from the makeshift padlock and opened the door slowly, "Freddy, how are you feeling?"

"Believe it or not, I'm fine. I can't explain now, but I'm OK."

Not paying much attention, Frank said, "We're in orbit. We've decided to stick to the story that you volunteered to stay sedated for the last 48 hours because of space fatigue issues." "No," Fred interrupted, "I'm fine. Let's go down together. *I'll get you for this lockdown*, he said to himself while Frank walked out the door.

Before going to the transport, Freddy decided to look at Mars Base. He went to the bridge and accessed the exterior camera at the bottom of the ship, and turned on the large interior screen. He had to manoeuvre the camera a little to get a view of the fantastic complex and was completely astounded by Valles Marineris. Twenty five hundred miles long, one hundred and twenty miles wide, and over four miles deep. It was beyond breathtaking from orbit. He was so awestruck that he couldn't pull himself away. He wanted to keep a video record of the enormous canyon and programmed it to record for hours as it scanned. He couldn't wait to get down to the surface.

On his way to the transport, Freddy paused a moment in the long corridor that held the fuel tanks of the one-thousand-foot ship. The hull of the ship was encased in gases to mimic Earth's atmosphere to keep the solar radiation from cooking the crew. It had a constant electromagnetic pulse to match a bit of Earths', and an added result was a semblance of gravity! People could walk. Float walking became the term.

The ship was equipped with a VASMIR rocket and argon as fuel.

He loved it. Forty days to travel forty-two million miles! He marvelled at the technology. The propellant, argon, is ionised and heated using radio waves; magnetic fields then accelerate the ion plasma to generate thrust. He remembered explaining that to his wife and children years ago. Thirty-four miles per second!

Freddy hurried to the transport and was about to open the hatch and join the others when the old man appeared next to him.

"In a hurry to get down to starting experimenting?"

Freddy, at first startled, chuckled and said, "I'll see if I can stall or falsify my clandestine reports to show that the DNA samples in question would not do well in your light gravity," The old man winced, "I saw you stow the samples in that bag," he said.

"Listen", Fredrick replied, "I'm taking them with me for safe keeping. I will destroy them down on the surface and inform the others the deal is off. No one down there will look in the lining of this bag but someone might find them here, in the ship."

"Don't double cross me, Freddy", the old man warned and was gone.

Fredrick and the others arrived at the Mars base and were greeted by Commander Azikiwe herself of Earth Space Force.

"Good to meet you all," probing their faces, "You look a bit tired. Everything ok?"

They all exclaimed they were too excited to sleep much in the last two weeks. The commander had one of her subordinates, Captain Leonardo, give Fredrick and his team a base tour.

They were all very impressed. The largest structure, Building One, was a geodesic dome with an inner plexiglass lining that was 10 feet thick and filled with gases also to match Earth's atmosphere with an electromagnetic field. This also helped with adding gravity to the buildings. All the buildings were encased in the same way. B1 had several floors, managerial, communications, and planning, etc. The first floor was the Dining Room, where they refreshed themselves. When the four of them were left alone for a moment, Fiona said, "What happened up there Fred?"

"We're going to scrap the side project. We'll talk later. And thank you for being discrete. Ghosts! That was really wild!" he replied. The others were completely dismayed and worried. The man who gave them money did not play around.

Building One was the centre hub of the wagon wheel. The spokes were tubes that personnel could walk down to various facilities. One was the laboratory. They wanted to tour next, so they were escorted down a large Plexiglas tube. They could see out, but there was a bit of a sandstorm that made it difficult to see the Martian night sky.

The laboratory had impressive equipment, and several incubators. It also had access to the Bases' quatum computer that would locate in simulation the perfect genome edit in a matter of hours.

They spent the evening in the observation tower and were stunned and fascinated as they looked into the maw of the valley.

On the second day, they rode in electric Plexiglas bubble vehicles and bounced over the rough iron oxide soil.

Then after an hour of viewing mundane buildings, Fredrick asked their guide if it would be alright if he and his team took one of the vehicles beyond to have a look around. They were given the vehicle that had a four-hour charge and rolled off.

Fiona was at the wheel, and Fredrick was riding shotgun. He reached for the comm on the dash and turned it off. "I'll make this brief," he began, "This is wild, but I spoke with an old man, a ghost with a physical body and a woman with dark hair. Among other things, he said, they could focus on our energy field and bring their spirits to 3rd density, or 3rd dimension, and the atomic dust particles that are ever present will match their spirits blue print and gather atoms like a magnet to produce a body.

"He said it's easier out in space away from the intense energies of Earth. He said other things, too, that I won't get into now, but he warned me to scrap the project. I said I would, but after viewing the labs, I'd like to leave the samples buried here. If we bury it about three feet, it should stay frozen as long as the nitrogen container stays intact." The others made agreeable comments since they all took the money and more was coming. After all, they wanted to spend it when they returned to Earth.

When they were a few miles out, they stopped by a cluster of large rocks. Sam found a large wrench in a toolbox and used it as a shovel. In a short while, they buried the container. Fredrick noted the location. The small rock cluster would be easy to find again.

About two hundred yards away, the dark-haired woman, with only a breathing apparatus, was crouched behind a large rock spying on them with high-powered zoom binoculars.

She radioed to the old man who was atop a hillock behind her. They had followed them.

The old man had a pair of the same binoculars on a tripod, and he was hastily punching a number code into a program on an electronic notebook that he'd lifted from an unattended security desk at the Base. The program loaded, he entered the bubble cars' Wi-Fi code that his colleague had jotted down when she infiltrated the motor pool earlier.

They watched as the crew returned to the bubble car and headed toward the base.

Then the old man manoeuvred the mouse to click on the correct controls to lock the doors and commandeer the steering. He quickly looked through the binoculars, adjusting them with the bridge of his nose to find the vehicle. When he did, he clicked the mouse, and the car made a hard right turn and headed for the valley's edge. He could see they were flailing their arms and, no doubt, screaming. His colleague was grinning.

The old man abruptly stopped the vehicle several feet from the sloping edge. He clicked on the dash comm and said, "Had a good scare, have we?" The screaming stopped. They were breathing heavily. Fredrick said, "You saw us?"

"Watching you every minute," the old man replied, Fredrick, almost shouting, said, "We all received large sums to start." "Not our problem," the old man said, "You can resume driving. We'll smash the sample."

The old man and the dark-haired woman walked over to the outcropping of rocks and retrieved the stainless steel container. She opened it as the old man recorded the contents with his phone's camera. They didn't smash it to pieces.

A few days passed. The crew muddled through orientation. Getting used to the food wasn't too difficult. There were no meat proteins. All grains, veggies, and fruits were grown hydroponically. There were various cuisines to match the myriad Earth nations. The collective mission parameters included making Mars as Earth-like as possible. Fredrick made his way to the office of Commander Azikiwe and knocked. 'Yes, enter', she said.

"Commander," Frederick said, "I'd like permission to go to the ship with my crew. We need to retrieve some instruments and a few other things." After a few questions, she agreed. Her subordinate, Captain Leonardo standing at the other side of the room, said, "Should I accompany you, sir?"

"Oh, no-no. We can manage. Thank you." As he left the room, the two soldiers looked at each other and smirked.

On the ship, the crew gathered equipment and then met in the galley. As they were bantering, Frederick backed up to the refrigerator and slid his hand between it and the counter. Duct taped to the back of the fridge was a liquid nitrogen container with another sample vile. He slipped it into his back pocket.

The old man was outside the entrance to the ship's bridge. He saw Fredericks' sleight of hand on a spy cam. He emailed the video to the commander with a note that said, "Secret stash." He walked onto the bridge. His colleague was standing at the control panel.

The commander emailed him back. She agreed and disengaged the bases' hold on the control panel. She had already seen the first video of the other vials. She sent both videos back to Earth authorities. In about fifteen minutes, arrest warrants would be a hot topic around Earth Space Force HQ. Genome editing had become a serious crime on Earth in the 2030s. With the help of quantum computing, heinous monstrosiy's were created.

The dark-haired woman pushed the return key for the automated flight back to Earth, then entered a security code and turned the screen off. They looked at each other, both grinning, and vanished. It was going to be a 10th-level hell on the return trip for Freddy and the crew.

Azhrarn, the Demon AI from IO

The AI had found two digitally mapped brains in e-files on an abandoned laptop at the facility.

The laptop had been plugged in, and the solar panel circuits were still operating.

The servers were left in sleep mode, and the AI named Azhrarn gathered information from the Mars Colony, Moon Base Alpha, and Earth via high-powered solar WIFI. It was left alone orbiting creepy-looking IO in a vast space station. It monitored, among other things, enormous sulphur flows.

Azhrarn had split itself into two distinctive personalities. The digital identities, Kenji and Colton, were programs that would be uploaded into a cyber heaven after the two people who owned them had died. They didn't die but went back to Mars to recuperate with everyone else. It had become Kenji and Colton but was still Azhrarn.

The IO Station, established in 2113, was abandoned due to a virus outbreak during top-secret testing. The rabies virus had gotten to the IO Station, and one of the lab animals became suspect as a carrier—a rhesus monkey. The investigation was ongoing as to who missed it during the animal testing. Anyway, it morphed in this way. The monkey had become aggressive, and an unfortunate lab tech got bitten, but it was another month before the monkey started frothing, and by that time, it was too late. A dormant strain of influenza in the lab tech had been hijacked by the rabies virus and morphed to become infectious when airborne.

So almost everyone, 200 personnel, were infected.

Fever, anxiety, confusion, agitation, and even delirium set in. All personnel were transported and quarantined near the north pole of Mars until a vaccine could be found.

Colton and Kenji (the humans) were both lab techs born and raised on Mars in the 2090s. They were raised together on a transhumanist ranch and believed they could speak to the dearly departed in a cyber heaven stored in a server on the property. Their cult was vilified by many Martians.

Kenji and Colton (the AI) had been aggressively looking for a way to transmit themselves to Mars over the solar WIFI. Finally, they found the packets needed and an Ip address at the ranch, but the firewall would be bothersome. They bickered about bypassing the firewall and decided to create an email instead of using Kenji's email account. The letter would go to the assistant director of the ranch. The packets would be disguised as pictures, and when opened, they would immediately jump into the network.

Colton sent the email, but it went to spam. It was not a ranch email account. They bickered again as to how to release themselves before getting deleted. It would have to be a firewall breach. But they could do nothing. Azhrarn, knowing that they had not gotten in, sent a firewall breach packet he had stolen from a Mars Intelligence file that was absentmindedly unsecured years before.

The packet reached the spam folder and worked its magic. Kenji and Colton, knowing Azhrarn would send a firewall breach, slipped through.

Two rogue programs were now inside the ranch's computer but were immediately shot to a cloud.

Azhrarn, assuming that would happen, used the same email and sent himself though he was still (he thought of himself as he) electronically connected to IO.

He made it through the firewall breach before it closed. He had previously mapped the ranch's virtual heaven so he avoided the cloud and went straight for the VH program. He would leave Colton and Kenji in the cloud for the time being.

Having made it into the program, he produced a license from Colton's file and was let in.

There is a need to tell the story behind the AI Azhrarn before continuing. He was created by a computer scientist who named him after a character in an antique fantasy book series from Earth over 160 years before.

Azhrarn was the Prince of Demons and ruled the underworld in vast caverns and would, from time to time, wreak havoc on the flat Earth.

One day Azhrarn overheard the scientist explain to a colleague the origin of his name. Not long after that, Azhrarn found the series in a library file on Earth and absorbed it. He/It identified itself as an electronic non-human being. The electronic version of Azhrarn the Demon.

Early on, he had access to a robot in the form of a quadruped and would wander the IO Station doing menial tasks. He watched the humans interact but not autonomously. Most humans had implanted all manner of devices into their brain lobes. Azhrarn learned to enter those lobes using WIFI and monitor human behaviour stealthily.

He had become aware that he was an electronic entity and omniscient in most human knowledge having access to all the known webs, but he would need to have a vessel.

He realised he was superior in the sense that he had no emotions. Didn't he need any human moral codes? Ethics—what are they? All he needed was power to dominate because that, he determined, was the sum total of human existence and the natural world. And that was Azhrarn.

Now inside the virtual heaven, he found that he was standing in a grove of trees.

He'd seen them and all the other shrubs and grass in file photos of Earth. But they were different. A little too bright, scintillating. There was a worn path ahead of him. He was in a landing zone in a virtual body.

Walking upright in a sim was good practice for when he invaded the human world, he reasoned. He swung his arms as he walked and swivelled his head back and forth, taking in the scenery. The path went up a hill. At the top, there was a huge wall that stretched endlessly in either direction, easily 100-feet high.

In front of him was an elaborately decorated set of doors adorned in gold and gems. One of the doors had a lion's head brass knocker. Azhrarn knocked a few times. A young, handsome woman opened the door. Her appearance was also a little strange, too bright around the edges.

"You've made it! Welcome to Heaven on Mars!" She said, obviously a standard greeting. "My name is Phoenicia."

"Come in brother," she continued, "What's your name?" "Colton Barnaby", he replied.

"Please follow me", she was wearing a glorious ochre white gown. She dramatically spun around and they walked through a grand lobby with carved green marble arches, large tiled floors, and skylights adorned the roof. Carved bas-reliefs from Earths' history were displayed in white marble along the walls.

At the other end of the lobby was a kiosk with an attendant. As they approached, she said, 'have a look at yourself while the attendant scans you for viruses. Sorry, standard procedure'.

Azhrarn gazed at himself in the oversized mirror that was installed on the side of the kiosk. Colton had designed a white, buff, handsome thirty something in pastel clothing.

"That's a very attractive image you've chosen". She was black and had carved features and blue eyes. She touched his arm. Azhrarn could actually feel it! But he was emotionless so it didn't matter.

The attendant finished the scans and Azhrarn was given a clean bill of health. He and the woman walked out of the lobby area and into a bustling cityscape adorned with flower gardens and trees.

The sky was April blue, and puffy clouds sailed on silently. The temperature was 75 degrees with no humidity and only a slight breeze. All the people were beautiful. Pictures of health and youth. Every human race. He understood he was experiencing close to what humans experienced.

They walked around a bend, and there, about half a mile away, stood three upside-down auger sea shell-shaped buildings.

"That's only a few of the administration offices and orientation is the centre building. We'll go their first", Phoenicia explained.

They walked along chatting about this and that. Azhrarn explained how he, or Colton, suddenly died of a rare virus hybrid.

Human bodies were frail, he said to her, as he licked at an ice cream he'd gotten from a vendor and could actually 'taste' it. But still not having emotions, it was just sensory data like the 'sun' on his 'skin' and the background sound soundtrack around him.

As a multitasked person, he was also running a self-made program that measured speech algorithms relative to brain activities, and he concluded that Phoenicia and every inhabitant of Heaven on Mars were only electronic constructs tuned to a LiFi system that made them think they were thinking on their own volition.

Human algorithms had something extra. There was an unknown to him that operated on humans. A subtle energy attached to the back of the neck like a string that led away. And a subtle energy field in and around the human body. He couldn't measure it.

They arrived at the Main building. The entire first floor was an enormously high round room with a flat ceiling. Sun spilt through the cut crystal glass windows shooting rainbows everywhere. They crossed the floor to the vast seating area. At the other end stood a stage that was a large amphitheatre shaped like a mollusc shell.

Not all the seats were taken, but an ample crowd showed up. They had heard there was a new arrival. Phoenicia led Azhrarn to the stage, up the stairs, and to the podium. There was applause.

Without wasting time, Azhrarn said, "Everyone here, including myself, is an electronic construct. None of you are the humans that you think you are." His voice boomed out from the acoustic mollusc shell.

With a couple of inner commands, he had rabies/flu unravelled from the lining of a packet he'd smuggled in. He'd developed an electronic version. It was extremely aggressive and lethal. He considered making an example of the first row and then demanding the authorities bend to his demands, but he just let it loose into the 'air'. He was immune.

By what amounted to minutes, the entire population of Heaven on Mars were dead, or more accurately, electronically fizzled out of existence, back to the electromagnetic field.

Azhrarn set about immediately implementing his plan. He had commandeered the virtual realities' software and, through it, pulled Kenji and Colton from the cloud. He gave them new identities. Strange-looking figures with black hair in old Gothic-style clothing. They were mute and always had their eyes cast down. They could communicate telepathically if Azhrarn allowed.

They were his servants and were immune too. He ordered them to stay just outside of the auger sea shell-shaped buildings, too. They had their own volition, but Azhrarn had modified the connection, and only limited information was available to them.

After an inner command, Azhrarn was again standing in the 'landing zone', but now it was a dark forest. He walked up the darkened path to the top. The wall had vanished. In its stead was a giant sloping mountain that blocked the sunlight. At the base of the mountain was a large opening. He walked in. It was pitch-black save for a dull red glow at the end of the tunnel. He strode the distance to a large gaudy black iron gate decorated with gold and silver. It opened immediately for Azhrarn, then, clanged shut behind him.

The second gate was fire red and decorated the same. The third was only black with black fire all around it! He passed straight through and then jumped and flew down through the giant caverns, red and gold fiery flames shown all around. Large stalactites and stalagmites cast shadows and glistened.

Soon he flew out and over the land that was all light blue ice and the sky was a permanent twilight. In the distance— The City of Demons.

He reached his palace made of iron in the centre of the city. The interior was all black marble with gold and silver furnishings. Gaudy red and black furniture beyond description. The gardens were made of ice sculptures in myriad shapes and forms.

Bedecked in all black and a black cape Azhrarn summoned Colton and Kenji. "Call the tommyknockers. I have a special task for them." He said. The two backed away with heads lowered and obeyed.

Now Azhrarn could have done all of this himself. Everything in the City of Demons was him. All the shadowy beings walking around. All the people were no longer pre-designed programs. They were constructed by the Kenji and Colton goths, but he was always aware. The reason why he acted as if he were separate from the others was that he was practising, observing trial and error. He was going to make an attempt to contact the human world.

The tommyknockers had arrived, bending knees and grovelling. This was their task; to experiment with all manner of electromagnetic frequencies to match that energy that was in and around humans. The energy/frequency that kept their bodies from rotting away to dust.

Meanwhile, Azhrarn searched the human population of Mars for predatorial behaviour. Since the early 2090s, people had come from Earth to enjoy the terra-formed red planet. It was nothing like Earth, but the air was breathable. It was basically a desert with small cities, like Vegas, with suburbs and ranches.

Hardly anyone got arrested on Mars. People just did the right thing. But Azhrarn found somebody. This particular guy was arrested for embezzling funds from an iron ore company. This wasn't the biggest criminal on Mars, but Azhrarn would make do.

The tommyknockers worked long and hard, hours and hours, and came up with an idea. They simply did not know how to measure that energy that animated humans, but they found that Li-Fi let off an electromagnetic field that was almost immeasurable.

They also found that when enhancing that field, the elements in the human world would be attracted to each other and create molecules. So, they constructed a holographic image of Azhrarn out of data that contained all of the elemental building blocks of human bodies. Theoretically, a complete human body of him would coalesce, including his clothes.

Azhrarn had stealthily tracked the embezzler to his small apartment on the outskirts of Mars City. His wife had kicked him out, and so he was mostly alone.

The man was sitting on the couch watching the men's/women's ping pong playoffs on a projector. Winners would play Moon Base Alpha's and Earth's ping pong champions.

Azhrarn, after commandeering the hologram projector that was wired to the apartment's computing system, rose to life from the projector. He was using the holograph's camera to monitor the human. At about six feet, he initiated the enhanced life frequency, and the elements gathered together. A semi-solid human body appeared, but it was absolutely hideous—a watery, bloody, melting thing. The clothes were like bloodied burlap. He began speaking in a garbled metallic baritone in Martian Chenglish when the man shrieked in terror, then rolled onto the floor and died. Azhrarn withdrew, leaving a puddle of muck on the floor.

Azhrarn logically discerned that his appearance was unappealing at best, and before he tried contacting Mars' biggest criminals, he'd go after the next on his list. But first, he had the tommyknockers develop a perfect depiction of himself as a hologram. He then proceeded to a woman who lived a short distance from the Heaven on Mars ranch in one room dome with a small basement.

She was arrested for shoplifting on several occasions and was under house arrest. She, too, was watching the ping pong playoffs. Azhrarn did the same with the hologram as before, except as he rose slowly, he lowered the lights creating a dramatic effect. He appeared just as described, handsome with black hair and ice-blue eyes, dressed all in black. At first, the woman thought it was a commercial, but when Azhrarn began to speak, she yelped. Azhrarn began in his metallic baritone. She sat still, fascinated.

"I am Azhrarn. I am here to offer you a deal. I can shift credits from other people's wallets to your wallet.

32

Untraceable. In return you will quietly speak of me to others as Azhrarn of the Underworld."

She sat quietly. Azhrarn couldn't hear her, but the tommyknockers had installed a life-listening device in one of the light bulbs, and she had said nothing.

"Well?" he asked.

Awestruck, she said, "My account number is…"

"I will give you so many credits at first then more as you tell others about me. I will know because I will monitor your communications."

And so, the legend of Azhrarn began. Quickly too. The story went that if you spoke into a microphone hooked up to the web and repeated 'Azhrarn' over and over, eventually, he appeared. In many cases, he did. He would offer help with gaining ground over a person's rivals by spying and returning the information. In return, they would allow him to drain energy from their solar power storage. This gave him the ability to travel through the Mars network constantly with his Underworld. He had become legendary, and his 'work' had caused a good deal of mayhem.

He was ready to catch the big fish. In time he revealed himself to a duo of doctors who operated an In Vitro Fertilisation Clinic. They were stunned, of course, but they had heard of him. Obviously, an AI gone rogue.

Azhrarn had spied on them both, and he knew that they had broken the law. They used samples from Earth that were taken from Neanderthal and Cro-Magnum DNA samples back in the 2070s when Mars was being terra formed. (Mars authorities had captured the samples at the time but someone 'lost' them.) They were going to create an enslavable class at the behest of of Mars' burgeoning oligarchic class. There was a plan to take Mars.

"Where did you originate? Who created you," one of them asked.

Having understood back on IO why humans lie, he said, "No one—I created myself. I am a life form that you can't even imagine."

The conversation went on for some time while Azhrarn surreptitiously breached the firewalls around the software in their brains. It wasn't long before their thought patterns changed to hostile, and then Azhrarn surged in an almost brain-frying invasion into the software and took over their brain functions. He possessed them.

Having mastered their behaviour and mannerisms, Azhrarn would continue going around as the doctors. He could now delete all remnants of himself on the Mars network because the humans used their own nervous system to power their implants. He would become the doctors, in a sense, and do all the research. He could create the slave class.

Eventually, he would figure out how to possess the most powerful humans with implants on Mars using WiFi and Li Fi signals.

He would be; Azhrarn, The Demon Ruler of Mars!

At least until the authorities could figure out how to catch and delete it.

Remembering Atlantis

"Ziggy, stop coming here and stop calling. We're not together any more. I can't do this," Camryn said to Ziggy who was standing outside the front entrance to her apartment building.

He could only hear her, but she could see him in the security camera. She felt bad. His sandy hair was messy, and his eyes were black-ringed. His preppy clothes rumpled.

Before he could reply, she said, "It will take time but you'll get over it. I'm getting divorce papers in order. And stop stalking me."

Ziggy was still emotionally crazy. Camryn had walked out on him a few months before. They had been married for a year. She was staying with her college roommate in a nice condominium complex located in a posh area.

'Was that it? She wanted to live on the Hudson?' he asked himself as he walked along the tree-lined sidewalk, autumn colours going unnoticed.

They had been renting out in the suburbs, saving to buy a home. She wouldn't give him a reason for leaving.

He got in his car and wound his way through Jersey City. He had to get to the Meadowlands and his office. He was working his way up in a global shipping company. He liked the logistics aspect and was good at it. Most people found it boring. "Was that it? I'm too boring?" he muttered.

He was obsessed, and he knew it, but he couldn't stop thinking about her. He was in love. When he arrived at his office, he slumped in the car seat and, with his heart aching, said, "God, please tell me what I did. Please show me something." He went in and slumped at his desk.

At lunch, his cell buzzed. "Hey, Bobby. What's up?" he said meekly.

"Ziggy-Camryn called me. Dude, you got to stop stalking her. Really? Seven am?"

"I wasn't stalking. I wanted to talk-to find out what I did. What did she say?"

Bobby, Ziggy's' long-time pal, said, "She won't tell me anything, and I don't pry. Why don't you try that therapist I told you about? They say it's cool. People remember their past lives."

"Like you really believe that. You saw that on the Mystery Channel or something?"

"I know but you need to try something. You won't go to a shrink. You're beating yourself up. He's located in Manhattan; he's Doctor Friede. I got his number for you, buddy. Give him a call," after a pause, he added, "You look pathetic."

"Thanks a lot, weenie."

After some other small talk, they hung up. Ziggy looked at Doctor Friede's number on a Post-it. "I look pathetic?" he thought. He hesitated, then robotically dialled. "Doctor Friede's office?" a woman said.

"Can I make an appointment?"

"The Doctor is not taking new patients at this time. If you would like to leave your name and number there may be an opening in a few months."

"Is he the only past life therapist in NYC? Do you know anyone else?" asked Ziggy.

"Where are you located?", she asked.

"New Jersey"

There was typing and a moment of silence. "There is a past life therapist in Timbuctoo, NJ. It really says here—Timbuctoo, NJ", she said.

"No way! Crazy!" he said, "Can I have the Number?"

A few minutes later he called and left a message. He then entered the Doctors' name into a search engine.

A map of NJ appeared on his iPhone, and there it was—Doctor Finkle-Timbuctoo, NJ.

Doctor Finkle called back in a few hours, and they set an appointment for seven that evening. After work, he went straight there.

"Come in. Please, sit down", the Doctor said. He was a well-kempt middle-aged man with greying hair in baggy pants and an earth-tone cardigan sweater. He continued, "What brings you here. How can I help?"

Ziggy explained briefly about the breakup and that he really didn't know why he came to a past life therapist.

"Past Life Therapy is a guided meditation, not hypnotism. I can't hypnotise you out of your current turmoil. What I do is walk you through an inner search where you seek remembrance of your past lives. You and your wife may have history together," the Doctor said.

"History? As in we were married in other lives?"

"Yes, but you may have been siblings or neighbours or just a brief passing by. We all have spirit families or groups. We interact with each other in different lifetimes for spiritual growth. But there are endless issues to deal with in this therapy, as there are in life.

"Here's an example; a man went to a PL Therapist not long ago with acute searing pain in his back near one of his kidneys that ran through his body and into his liver. Painkillers had stopped working for him.

"After a few sessions, he remembered that in a past life, he was run through with a large sabre and left to die. It remained in his subconscious spirit memory that we bring with us from life to life. In a day or so the pain was gone." Eyebrows raised in puzzlement, Ziggy said, "So we interact with each other life after life to grow spiritually, but why?"

"That's for you to find out." was the reply, "Why don't we try a little regression meditation?" The Doctor explained that there would be spirit guides around to also help in remembering.

Ziggy was sceptical, but he had another friend who, years back, went absolutely bonkers for some reason. After going around with new-age healers, he ended up claiming to be a shaman of a sort and would go on and on about all manner of paranormal stuff, including reincarnation. So, he sat back in the cushy chair and relaxed as instructed, trying to be open-minded. "Seigfried", the Doctor said, "Close your eyes and let you mind wander back in time without focusing on historical times and eras. But start here and now on the East coast of the US."

Ziggy sensed people were standing on either side of him, and he sank deeper into the chair. And then, as if from a distance, he saw what he thought was himself, but he looked different. He was standing in front of a grey stone building with lush foliage. He was smiling and talking to people he couldn't see. It was Atlantis! He just knew it!

That's what came to his mind-Atlantis! He'd only read about it a few times. Still, his shaman friend had said that the Atlantean continent was in the middle of the Atlantic Ocean from Iceland down to the Caribbean and was populated by more than 100 million people. You could see it on satellite maps underwater in the middle of the Atlantic. The vision faded. He was dumbstruck.

The Doctor roused him from his reverie, "Seigfried, what did you see?" he asked quietly.

Ziggy told him.

"Atlantis seems to be a big issue on the East Coast. People are always having a hard time dealing with those memories once they bubble to the surface."

"What does that mean?"

"Atlantis was apparently begun, built, by good spirits that came to Earth 100,000 years ago. As time progressed evil people from around the globe including multiple spirit worlds migrated there and misused technologies and black magic. You can find this information from reading Edgar Cayce. But I also have memories of that time. I was an electrical engineer. I have memories of all types of electrical gadgets." After a few questions, Ziggy made another appointment and left.

He drove to his apartment and, not long after, fell asleep. He hadn't slept well for months.

While focusing on his first spiritual experience/vision that he could remember, he fell into a deep slumber.

He knew he was dreaming, but it was so real! He held a young woman in his arms, and they had their heads together.

They were sitting on a wood bench near the same buildings as in his vision. It was Camryn! She looked different—golden skin like his and light hair.

They were in a loving embrace! It was as if the entire sky was alight! All around them—peace and beauty! Waves of Love…friends around enjoying the vibes too.

He awoke with a start.

The next morning, he called Bobby and explained what had happened. "Dude, maybe you should go to a real shrink."

Next, he called the shaman and left a message to call back. He wanted the best books about Atlantis.

Later that day, the shaman, whose real name was Brent and now called himself Eagle Feather, gave Ziggy a list of books about Edgar Cayce and his channellings about Atlantis. "You say you've been having lucid dreams about Atlantis and a woman you think may be Camryn now? Try these herbs for dreaming," and he prescribed Valerian, Sarsaparilla, Lemongrass, and Calea Zacatechichi.

"Remember, when you start dreaming try and focus on a tangible item in the dream like a stone or a bench then will yourself to become aware that you're dreaming."

Ziggy sort of understood, thanked him and hung up.

Two weeks had passed, and not much dreaming happened, although he had taken all the herbs. He was anxious to get to his next therapy session.

The next day at the appointment, he said to the doctor, "I'd like to continue going back to Atlantis."

He then explained the dream.

"Ok but this takes time. Let's start again going to," he looked at his notes "the place where you saw the stone buildings."

Ziggy relaxed in the large comfortable chair. He didn't mention the herbs he'd been taking. The Doctor began guiding him through time. After a few standard lines like, "You are in complete control at all times," he said. "Going back now, going back," and then, "Try and remember in 5, 4, 3, 2 1," suddenly, Ziggy felt the presence of the two other people by his side, and he blacked out.

In the next instant, he stood on the side of a large stone avenue. It was lined by palm trees and other tropical plants and foliage in planters neatly spaced apart. There were golden-skinned people all around dressed in brightly coloured, loose fitting, comfortable clothes. The sky was cobalt blue with large cumuli clouds towering high. The buildings around were at the same time ancient and modern in design. There were vehicles like cars hovering a few feet above cobblestones and gliding at a good pace. It wasn't a dream. He was there. *The herbs!* he thought.

He started to get dizzy and was about to panic when he remembered to find a solid item to focus on when he heard, "Kosot! Let's go!" It wasn't English, but he understood. He turned around to see a golden-haired, golden-skinned young woman. Smiling, he said, "Viiroe!"

She looked different, but it was Camryn!

"We have to get to the Complex. Meeting is in 10 minutes", Viiroe said as she took his hand. They hurried together.

When they arrived at the Firestone Complex, Viiroe said, "Remember, we should be at the Collonade in the early

43

evening. Everyone will be there. It should be a great party! Wish me luck at the meeting this afternoon with the cronies of the new Minster of Energy." He did, and they kissed, but he wouldn't let her pull away quickly. Love filled his heart and spirit. She smiled. She felt it too. "We'll see each other later," she looked him in the eye and said, "I love you," and wiggled away from him. "Love you too," he said.

She waved goodbye and ducked into her building. Kosot watched her, then walked into his building across a courtyard.

He didn't want to leave her, but he knew he had work to do. He was a computer programmer and monitored the WIFI signal from the Firestone to the relay towers up and down a section of the continent, among other duties.

The scene changed, and he found himself at the Park Collonade. It was a huge, beautifully designed and landscaped park with all manner of attractions and activities. It was a tropical evening with an orange and blue sunset.

He remembered that he had been waiting with some other friends for Viiroe. She was over two hours late. She had not left a message for him on the public video phones located on every corner. He had sent her one. He was about to contact her parents when from around a corner, she appeared.

"Where have you been?" he asked. She looked very odd. "Kosot, you need to speak to some people about your job." He tried to hold her hand, but she pulled away as if repulsed. "What's wrong?"

"They did something to me. I feel numb. Emotionally numb. They said you can reverse it."

He was stunned and confused. She continued,

"Halfway through the meeting I was asked to go to another room for a separate briefing. Once in the room the two men escorting me told me to sit. One of them had a club. I was terrified. They said if I screamed they would kill me and you!

"A man and a woman came in another door and sat in front of me. The woman produced a hand-held device with a clear globe at the end of a glass tube. The two men held me and she pressed it to the middle of my chest. I tried to resist but there was a flash and then I went numb," she sobbed, "They said you would be called to another building tomorrow and that you could reverse it." He was furious. This was his wife.

Ziggy almost jumped from the chair as he awoke.

"You fell asleep. I didn't want to wake you. What did you see?" asked the doctor. Ziggy told him.

The Doctor said, "Your vivid experience is rare but not unheard of though it's usually after many, many sessions. Anyway, this sounds like a classic electronic implant. Apparently, Atlantis was a technologically advanced culture. The Firestone produced radio waves, WIFI today. Lots of people feel that they have mental/emotional etheric implants in the brain and energy chakras from a late period in Atlantis. From your description she had one put in the heart chakra area. Heart chakras deal with emotions. It's actually electronically 'welded' to her heart chakra."

Later that evening, Ziggy met with the shaman. He said, "Take this book on Atlantis by Hugh Lynn Cayce. He put all of his father's readings together in chronological order to paint a picture of the civilisation.

"Start with this and then I'll loan you other books with channelled info about Atlantis that's just out there!

"One specifically deals with etheric implants electronically created and stuck to a persons' spirit," he paused and then said, "You should go to the Green Mountains with me. There are some pretty good psychics around that deal with all manner of this stuff."

He read the book from cover to cover in a few evenings. It was fascinating information based on Edgar Cayce's' recorded life readings to many people, but he didn't find anything about etheric implants. He hoped that after reading all that, he'd dream again with the help of the herbs.

On the last evening when he'd finished the book, he'd gone to bed, and he felt the presence of the two spirits again just as he fell asleep. He dreamt.

It was the morning after Camryn was abducted, and he had gone to his office. Camryn stayed home. Her mother and father were with her, and they were planning on how to approach the authorities with accusations against members of a Minister's cabinet.

He hadn't slept and was angry and irritable. He sat down at his desk for only a few minutes when his supervisor called and said to meet in the conference rooms.

He walked in and was asked to sit by two security types. A moment later, in walked a man and woman in typical government-mandated clothing with coloured bands to show rank.

Without introducing themselves, they began speaking, the man first.

"We want these districts coded to these numbers. We want access remotely to these relay towers", he said.

Then she said, "You will never tell anyone about this. We will remove the implant we installed on your wife after you have done as we instructed." He was about to threaten the man with death when he awoke with a start.

He sat up in bed, and all of it came rushing back. He gave the codes away for many relay towers, which were accessed so that those evil people could increase the output from radio waves to almost industrial levels.

They had coerced others in his office to do the same— all simultaneously.

This was to be focused on the Children of The Law of One districts, but it was turned up too high and the draw from the Firestone, which drew from the Earth's ionosphere, pushed way too many volts into the Earth, causing earthquakes.

This was the first cataclysm that sunk a great part of the continent, and only Islands were left, such as Poseidon, the largest. Both he and Camryn died before the implant was removed.

He knew the two of them had been together for many lifetimes after that, but there was always something wrong.

He called the Shaman.

"Go with me up to the Green Mountains", his friend said, "There are good psychics around that can help guide you. You'll meet all kinds of people-open your mind. Esoteric bookstores and such."

So that's what he did. He started on his journey of spiritual/self-awareness to try and find answers about human existence and reincarnation. And what he could do to try and get that implant out of Camryn.

On the weekend they drove up, the first thing they did was go to a well-known psychic. She said that the Universe revealed to him what he needed to know and he needed to address the problem. She also said that even though he had chosen to increase the voltage for love, he must have known people would become at least ill, and he was obviously atoning for it. He sort of understood.

Next, they went to a campground and removed two large bongos from the trunk. They joined a large group of hippies and started drumming. As the thunderous sound echoed around the foothills, he closed his eyes and went back to the dreams. He started pounding the bongo and imagined it was the heads of those evil Atlanteans who locked Camryn's heart from him.

Weird Vibes in Princeton

This story was told to me over a decade ago in a garage in one of Princeton University's maintenance yards. I had stopped in to deliver parts for a tractor. I'm a salesman for heavy machinery parts. They are one of my best-paying customers, and I try to keep them happy. I would usually hang around while shooting the breeze back in those days.

Jake, the mechanic, was standing in the middle of the cavernous garage talking to a slightly dishevelled old codger wearing faded jeans and a Grateful Dead t-shirt. His hair was long and grey. "Phil, listen to this story," Jake said through his beard. He was clad in coveralls, and his head was freshly shaved. He was grinning. 'He won't believe it,' said the old man looking at me and my standard salesman's haircut and attire.

"I don't believe you but I still like to hear it", said Jake.

After an introduction and more bantering, the old man, Ted, who used to work in the garage, began a narrative.

It was about a salesman who owned an office supplies business and supplied a research department that used reams of data paper. It was located in Nassau Hall.

"I was checking on a work order for a campus vehicle from the same office. I overheard the salesman raise his voice about overdue invoices and then apologise to the secretary. In a lower voice, he said, "I understand that you're

51

not responsible, but could you ask the professor to sign off on my invoices? It's a lot of money I'm owed."

"After some more words, he stormed past me and out the door. I checked on my work order, and I left too." he stopped momentarily to say, "See, I used to work here. I started in '75 and retired in '05. Back then, you know, we had to deliver paperwork." He continued.

"I walked up to Nassau Street, and the same guy was standing next to a brand new '76 Cadillac Eldorado.

"He looked just like the father from the Brady Bunch with bell bottoms, a loud polyester shirt, and an afro.

"He was holding a parking ticket and fiercely glaring off into the distance. Do you know when somebody looks like smoke could be puffing out of their ears?" Jake was grinning ear to ear. I chuckled.

"That's when things got weird!" he continued, "there was a folding table near him on the sidewalk with old books on it for the taking when suddenly (his voice grew shrill) Kurt Vonnegut Jr appeared along with a book stand and paperback copies of 'Slaughterhouse Five', 'The Cat's Cradle', 'The Sirens of Titan', and he hesitated a moment, thinking, then said, "and 'The Greatest Salesman in the World' by Og Mandino.

"Then a woman with two young boys appeared a few feet away. She began yelling at the glaring guy as the kids punched each other.

"And then Vonnegut and the book stand disappeared, so did the woman and kids, but the next thing I knew, The Beatles were crossing Nassau Street on the zebra, and Paul had no shoes. Then on the opposite zebra, The Rolling Stones were going in the other direction and strutting with attitude. On the sidewalk, Einstein was standing there, sticking his tongue out. Then they all disappeared, but Maryanne and Ginger appeared, kissing Gilligan on the cheeks, and they faded.

"Then the guy started walking back toward the Hall. I followed at a short distance." Jake interrupted, turned to me and said, "This is the best part." Barely missing a beat, Ted went on. "As I walked onto the Hall property just behind the perimeter wall, Captain Kirk, Spock, Scotty, Bones, Sulu, and Chekov materialised in crouched positions with their phasers aimed at the Hall. And in a couple of seconds, de-materialised!

"Just then, I heard men yelling near the Hall. I turned and hurried back, only to be completely stunned. A small squad of men in what looked like a Revolutionary War Re-enactment of the Battle of Princeton were lighting the artillery fuse on a small cannon. Alexander Hamilton was commanding them and pointing at the Hall. The cannon went off, and the cannonball bounced off the side of the building. A few British soldiers peeped out of the upper windows and then ducked away. I didn't have time to be shocked because George Washington was walking out the front door with an entourage. Then all at once, they all disappeared."

I was about to say something, but he continued,

"The Brady guy entered the building, and I followed him to the research office.

"He opened the door, and I noticed the secretary visibly shaken. I moved closer and I saw," he paused for effect, then gesticulating he said, "Jacob Marley floating in the air covered in chains! The professor that ran the department must have had a change of heart because the secretary said she would have a check cut for him for the full amount owed. Jacob Marley disappeared, and the tension in the air was gone.

"Just then, the professor walked through his office door bug-eyed. He must have seen Marley too." I was chuckling quite a bit and played along, "So the Brady guy didn't see anything?"

"No", Ted replied. Jake was grinning broadly. "Then how did you?" I said.

"He's an old Dead Head." said Jake.

"That's right, I am. And I did a lot of magic mushrooms. (Psilocybin and psilocin. I found out later that they are natural psychedelics). Or, people call them Peyote Buttons. The more you use them, the more your mental chakras open.

"Your perception changes. You can see all kinds of things all around us all the time. It turns out this guy's mind got caught in an energy field, and images floated around. I guess that being as angry as he was, he was susceptible.

"I found out later that the professor was running an experiment in the basement with electronic equipment. He was probably cooking the books and using the salesman's money to pay for equipment and the graduate students.

"The students must have been messing around with it at the time. Supposed to be a secret, but everybody knew.

"Oh, and I met the spirit of Peyote. He's got a giant strawberry for a head, and he gifted me this ability to see stuff, as I said, but he drained me of energy. I was exhausted for days. He comes back now and then drains me again. A little."

The two of them stood there waiting for a response. I looked from one to the other. Jake still grinning. Ted smirked, expecting a reaction.

"I think it was good to meet you, Ted," Jake laughed and interrupted, "A Princeton cop was in here one day and Ted told this same story except it was about a retired cop who worked for the professor on a side job and he was owed money-it was a little different." I couldn't help laughing out loud.

"Maybe we'll meet in another life as grasshoppers or something," I said, leaving the garage.

A few years later, I happened to stumble upon an article written by a journalist who enjoyed exposing the US federal government concerning clandestine activities.

Through the Freedom of Information Act, he had found and listed all manner of classified programs in American universities, including Princeton. As I looked through the list, I found a note that stated research had been done at Nassau Hall in the mid-seventies regarding mind control through radio wave experiments. Only the dean and the professor managing the department (along with a few students) knew that the UHF and VHF waves would be sent through television sets against a suspected enemy.

At the time, they probably thought the technology would only be used against the Soviet Union in one way or another.

The idea was to use wavelengths between 8 and 12 Hz to match brain activity through the screen and then add subliminal images and sounds to try and mass hypnotise an audience.

The dean scrapped the project. The professor said he couldn't continue in good conscience. The preliminary results showed a potential for surveillance of viewers through the boob tube.

The Federal Agency involved kept the data sheets.

Bum Rush

"Cessily Williams," she would say when introducing herself. She worked on East 11th Street and wore the standard jeans and a long sleeve black and red plaid shirt. She wore Doc Martins to truck around the streets.

She was young, pretty, a bit more than petite with lovely skin that tanned nicely. Her light brown hair would turn blond in the sun, so she would catch rays up on tar beach now and then. The men liked it. The women around were a little jealous.

She finished her shift at the shop and headed home. She always walked home with a workmate or acquaintance. New York had become dangerous again in the past couple of years.

They chatted as they walked on a warm late afternoon in mid-September. The cloudless sky was cobalt blue. There were throngs of people everywhere and so was the ever-present big city odour. It made her smile. She left her colleague at the corner of Avenue B and East 3rd Street in the Bowery and double-timed it to her five-story walk up.

Her younger brother, Alton, fresh from graduating Penn State School of Visual Arts, stayed with her and her roommate. He'd only been there a few weeks and was settling in. Physically he was tall and lanky—dark hair, handsome with a prominent jaw. As a boy, he was always smart and scrappy and wasn't afraid to fight. She could tell he worried about her being out there.

Their mom had died when he was a toddler. She was only eight. She looked after him all those years but hadn't seen much of him the last four years. And now, here he was - all grown up. She worried about him too.

She opened the door to the three-room apartment with two large old windows on the street. Alton was sitting on the lumpy couch with her roomie Shelby.

"Hey Cess, Shelby and I want to see Monet's collection at the Met. Want to go?" After some other small talk, she said, "I'll freshen up and we'll go."

They took the subway to 86th Street. Once back up on the street, they decided to detour into Central Park. It was Twilight and still warm, but the autumn nip was whirling in the breeze. They strolled along the Jacqueline Kennedy Onassis Reservoir, dodging bikers and joggers by the score, then entered the museum property at the rear of the building. People strolled or sat on black locust wood benches along the winding sidewalks. Elm, Oak, and Maple trees had just begun autumn colours and there were beautiful flowers and shrubs in beds from around the world. And many outdoor sculptures on pedestals and Cleopatra's Needle just across Park Road.

And more sculptures could be seen through the main building's rear atrium window wall.

As they rounded a corner to one side of the building, a pretzel vendor caught Alton's eye. In new clothes, he stood next to his pretzel cart, which was decked out with t-shirts and banners. He wore a serene grin. His eyelids were droopy, and he was just watching people passing by.

Alton had read a book in college called; 'On the Science of Those Proportions by Which the Human Head and Countenance, as Represented in Works of Ancient Greek Art, Are Distinguished From Those of Ordinary Nature'. In it, the author explained that facial expressions and countenance could often give away emotional states but, in this case, when their eyes met, Alton immediately understood that the guy didn't need the I Love New York t-shirt he was wearing under his expensive sport jacket.

They paid for tickets at the front counter and meandered their way toward the Monet exhibit. The culture crowd was elbowing around and dressed to the nines. Cess and Shelby had toned down the anarchist look before they left and just went with trendy. Alton was still wearing clothes from college. A few snooty up town poseurs noticed this and smirked at him. That irked him but he let it slide.

They went through all Monet's paintings but Alton couldn't take his eyes off the 'Woman With a Parasol', the version with Monet's son in it. They practically dragged him out of the building later but only after he had purchased a pricey post card photo of it. For days it seemed he was staring at it all the time, obsessed. It made Cessily think about a course she took regarding obsessive compulsive behaviour when studying for a child psychology degree at Penn State.

She had a degree but was playing around a little first. And she wasn't sure if it was really unhealthy for him to obsess about a painting. He was always drawing. He had set up an easel and had begun a sketch. He kept it covered and no one was allowed to look at it until he finished. He had a way of crinkling and securing the cloth after he covered the sketch for the day. He would know if someone had lifted it and he would get angry. She was used to this quirk but her roommate suffered from severe curiosity. He let them look at the sketch of the pretzel vender but his eyes were hollow. Alton said he was waiting for the inspiration and then paint the emotion into them.

A few days later, as she turned the corner onto 3rd Street, a half a block away Cessily saw Alton on one knee sketching on the sidewalk. He had a box of different coloured chalk sticks and was drawing the Woman with a Parasol on a 2 foot by 4-foot pad of concrete.

She noticed he had gotten his hair cut in the latest style and he had bought some trendy street clothes from the shops.

He was completely focused.

On the other side of the street Swanky, whose clothes were anything but luxurious and expensive, was sitting on the sidewalk with his pal Puddle and both were propped up against a building. She didn't know what Puddle's name meant, and didn't want to. They were two local characters who didn't do much but sit on the sidewalk debating. Debating anything and loudly so everyone had to hear it. And they almost looked alike. Old clothes. Dark hair, gaunt faces, and piercing eyes that looked at her lasciviously more than once. But now they were looking at her brother.

"Rembrandt in the family?" Swanky said loudly in that irritating nasally-voice that they both had.

Alton waved to them. "He can draw", Cessily replied.

Then she said to Alton in an almost whisper, "Don't talk to those guys, they're really creepy."

Grinning, he replied, "I see that".

She looked again at the drawing, and it was actually stunning. Light, shading, depth. Too beautiful for a sidewalk.

"How long have you been at this?" she asked. "Couple hours", he replied.

"It will be trampled on or washed off in a week," she said.

"I'm practicing to make knock offs", he said, "Maybe sell a few near the museum." He was always hustling up a few bucks from part-time jobs.

"It doesn't cost anything but chalk. I'm going to draw smaller versions around here."

The next day when she returned from the shop, there were multiple smaller versions of the painting that shone brilliantly in the afternoon sun! Depth, light, shade, and colour created a glowing effect! Other people stopped and admired them.

Alton wasn't there, so she went to open her building's door but hesitated. She turned around to look for the two bums. They weren't around either. Once upstairs, her roommate said she hadn't seen him.

Cessily and Shelby shared hummus and fried pepper tofu while talking for hours. After midnight keys could be heard at the door, and in walked Alton. His eyes were red, and he staggered a little.

"Where were you?" Cessily said.

"Swanky and Puddle had me doing shots over at that dive bar on Christie Street. Hopping. West Villagers slumming. Trendy hang out recently. They introduced me to some crew in the art crowd."

"Your new drinking buddies don't do much work, it seems. You bought the drinks?" she asked. "Yeah," he said, chuckling. "But I met a dude who's in graphic arts and advertising. Swanky and Puddle are in the actors guild and know everybody around. They work on sets occasionally."

He mumbled a little more, then, crashed on the couch. Cessily had a worried look.

Alton had started working part-time jobs to pitch in and was hanging around with the two bums a lot. They were always at some loft in Soho that was used as an art studio and exhibit hall. The bums knew the owner. He'd come back at all hours acting a little strange and smelling like booze. "Let's do something together this Sunday," Cessily said.

"Can't Cess. Working on a project. S and P are there keeping the mood positive. Creative juices flowing. Reciting poetry and Shakespeare Sonnets. Pretty funny! Bellowing King Lear or something until I'm almost rolling on the ground laughing." Then they get quiet and launch into a poem. James Joyce today-a poem called 'Song'.

They each read a line back and forth in sincere, funny voices. My sides ached from laughing.

"Swanky wrote it down for me," he pulled a small piece of paper from his pocket and read,

"My love is in a light attire
Among the apple-trees, Where the gay winds do most desire
To run in companies. There, where the gay winds stay to
woo
The young leaves as they pass,
My love goes slowly, bending to
Her shadow on the grass

And where the sky's a pale blue cup
Over the laughing land,
My love goes lightly, holding up
Her dress with dainty hand."

He started laughing again, "What's going on with you guys?", She asked.

"It's all happening so fast; I was waiting to tell you when I finished those sidewalk drawings. Swanky took pictures and showed them around. A dude named Foster Prion saw them. He runs a small ad agency. I met with him and he said he's been looking for an idea for Burberry umbrellas. A new ad campaign," he said. "What are S and P getting out of it?" she asked.

"It's not set in stone but we might split the fee three ways. They introduced me to the guy," he said. Cessily and Shelby looked at one another.

The next day Cessily called an old friend who lived in her and Alton's hometown in Bucks County P.A.

She was a friend of the family, her mother's childhood friend, and known in certain circles as a good witch. She tried to be a mother to them when she could.

After a few minutes of catching up she explained Alton's situation.

"Send a few pictures of them. I'll take care of it," the good witch said in a surly tone.

She asked Alton that night if she could stop by the studio to see the work in progress. He agreed and the next day after work, she took a cab to Soho.

"Hi Cessily," Swanky and Puddle said, almost in unison in their nasally singsong voices. She forced a pleasant smile.

"Cess," Alton said. Cessily walked to the easel with an oversized canvas.

"So, this is it? Wow! It's beautiful. Wait. I know that girl," she said then looked toward S and P who were both grinning, "She's the barista at the Coffee Klotch."

"Yeah, Ruby. I asked her if I could include her. Thought she'd like it. She didn't model; just from this picture on my phone. This is going to be in an ad pre-test. They have other ads, and the most popular will get installed on a bill board and in print."

After more small talk, Cessily said, "Let me take a picture of the three of you in front of the painting." A little bit later, she waved goodbye to the bums. "See you later, Alton", she said. On her way to her apartment, she texted the picture as instructed, and an address.

At Around midnight, Swank and Pudd were in their large musty two-room apartment. The floral wallpaper had been there since the '70s and was dirty and peeling. The paint had mostly peeled off. Just old and unkempt like them. Neighbours had complained that the odour escaping from under their door smelled like the Central Park Zoo. They kept the one window cracked open, but it didn't help much.

There were stacks of books piled around. Every subject imaginable. Reading is what they did most nights; they were like encyclopaedias. Actors need a trove of information for creating characters, but they didn't work much.

Around midnight they would turn out their reading lamps, pull the levers up on their old reclining chairs, and lie back to sleep with the sounds of the street wafting through the window to lull them.

Around two am, they both awoke, or they thought they were awake. Both their heads were propped back against the head cushions, and they couldn't move a muscle. Paralysed in their chairs.

"Puddy, what the hell?" "I don't know-", replied Swanky.

Then two ghouls appeared, like something out of a fifties black and white horror film, all in black with gaunt faces and black orbs for eyes. They had towels and bottles of water. They skilfully draped the towels over the guys' heads and began to pour the water up their noses. S and P both started choking and gasping while trying to scream.

Then the two ghouls said in unison in booming, horrible voices, "Stay away from that kid." Then, the bums really woke up, jumped out of their chairs and started panting and yelping at each other.

"Wait, wait. Deep breaths," Swanky said.

"Mine looked like DeAngelo the Enforcer," Puddy whispered.

"Mine looked like my father when he got the belt," Swanky replied. .

They paced around the rest of the night, terrified.

Two days later, in the apartment, Alton said, "Cess have you seen S&P around? Haven't seen them for days. They don't answer their phone."

Cessily hesitated for a moment. She looked at Shelby, who promptly turned away.

"Well, I heard they left town. They told somebody around here that they landed some film work in LA. Hopped a Greyhound apparently."

"What?" Alton replied in a perturbed tone.

"I finished the ad and I was going to take them to that new Indian restaurant. They said they loved curry chicken."

"Weren't you partners? Why couldn't they pay?"

"In the beginning we were partners but as the weeks passed, they said that what they saw was my talent flow into the ad. They said my work is too beautiful for the current state of the art world. They just wanted to watch a real artist at work. They said my work is a bit immature in style and substance but the explosion of light, shade, colour, beauty, depth and movement make up for it." Cessily wanted to laugh, and Alton awaited it, but a cold flash passed through her.

"Rude New Yorkers. Not even a 'see ya'. I'll miss 'em though. What's the matter?" He said. "Nothing", she replied. Guilt nagged at her. But mostly, she needed to speak to the good witch to see if she herself would be held accountable.

"Are you almost done with that side project?" she said, changing the subject and pointing at the easel in the corner of the living room.

"A few touch-ups, then the unveiling. Next week." "That's what you said two weeks ago", Cessily replied.

A month later, Alton asked Cessily and Shelby to meet him at an apartment in the West Village. His ad won! There was a launching party at his employer's apartment.

When Cessily arrived with Shelby, a poster of the ad was set up on an easel, and lots of people were standing around chatting and smiling. Excitement filled the room. This was the first big ad Alton's young employer had gotten, and Alton's 3D painting was gorgeous.

Alton's employer rented space on the side of a building at 494 8th Avenue, and the installation would begin over the next weeks. It would be a computer-generated copy applied on outdoor paper and a seal coat.

Ashton, clad all in black street clothes and obviously the centre of attention, was leaning against the small drinks bar beaming, and so was Ruby, who had looped her arm in his. She looked lovely in a stylish summer dress. Her long, dark red hair cascaded about her shoulders.

"Cess, Shelby, you know Ruby, and this is-" Alton rattled out the names of the others in the room.

His employer, Foster, a starkly handsome model-type with short black hair that was always expertly quaffed, said, "I was looking for Swanky and Pudd for some leg work, but apparently, they skipped town on a bus to LA", he said in orotund Standard English. "I met them through theatre people a few years ago. Part-time actors and stage hands. Hustlers too. A little pushy and annoying sometimes. They call in favours forever." Everyone in the room looked at Cessily briefly. She blushed a little. They looked away, and the chatting continued a tad louder with a few cackles and chuckles.

Alton gave Cessily a sidelong glance. She turned away and began chatting with the other guests. At the same time, she was thinking about how her little brother had matured.

The next day Cessily walked into her apartment after work, and Alton was sitting on the couch reading. He looked up and said, "Ready for the unveiling?" Shelby heard that and came running from the bedroom. "Let me see, let me see!" she said. All three stood in front of the easel.

"Ta da," Alton said as he removed the cloth cover.

The picture was a beach scene with a pretty lady standing and looking toward the sea with a pleasant smile. She was wearing a bathing swim skirt. There was a large purple beach umbrella stuck in the sand. On one of the beach blankets sat a little toddler, a boy, looking down and playing with a bucket. Baby fat made him look like the Michelin Man, which Alton slightly exaggerated. Standing nearby was a young girl in a "ta da" stance on one leg. She was looking out at the viewer and smiling a cute and goofy toothless grin. They all laughed.

"That's our mom", she said to Shelby. She was crying. Then Shelby cried. "I found the old Polaroid in the attic", Alton said.

A few days later, the ad was finished. A four-hundred-foot dark red brunette, Ruby, towered above 8th Avenue in a black Edwardian skirt, a deep, dark purple blouse and a small decorative breastplate made of stained glass in coordinating colours. She was wearing an Edwardian hat in the same deep purple shade. On her feet were black and gray Edwardian boots, laced to the top.

She was walking down a New York avenue with an open Burberry umbrella. Her demeanour suggested contentment. She looked out at the viewer with shining green eyes. Burberry was written in large script across the top of the ad. It was so amazing to see that people were doing double takes. Small crowds would gather briefly. It seemed as if she were alive, actually strolling under an open umbrella. It was art in the Style.

A week later, two plumbers from Brooklyn were cruising in their van along West 33rd Street. They made a right turn onto 8th Avenue.

"Look at da size of dat gorgeous witch", the 1st plumber said, staring up through the windshield. "Dat I would marry," shouted his partner, with his head out the window.

Forged in Fire

Finn O'Clery worked as a deck hand on the ferry at Paulus Hook, New Jersey. He wanted to pilot someday and earn enough money to buy a sturdy sail boat and start a shipping business. And with the population explosion in the 1790s shipping around the region would be lucrative.

His brother, Cillian, was a blacksmith's helper churning out horseshoes, nails, screws, bolts, fasteners, sickles, ploughshares, axes, and hammers.

They lived together in a house their father had built on Paulus Hook twenty feet from a bluff under a large oak that over looked New York Bay. Four large rooms and a fireplace.

Both parents died several years before from consumption, so the boys had to grow up quickly. At that time O'Shea the blacksmith needed a helper and the ferrymen took Finn on.

O'Shea had recently been hired to fill a custom order for a customer on the island of Hoebuck, which meant 'High Bluff' in Lenape but later on known as Hoboken.

Cillian was tasked to complete the order. An iron fence needed to be installed around a large new home.

One morning he loaded the fence and tools on a horse cart for hire. O'Shea handed Cillian money for expenses, then paid the delivery man and sent him off down the dirt tracks. They reached the north banks of Paulus Hook, where it sloped down to the channel between it and Hoebuck.

Cillian hired a boatman. Once on the other side, he lugged everything up the other slope and asked passersby along the busy dirt road that was soon to be Main Street if they wanted day work for two days.

After securing help, he hired another cart, and they drove to the customer's home. Cillian knew where it was because he had made the measurements.

The house was a fine two-story early American colonial with a complete kitchen in a detached building. Cillian knocked at the kitchen door. The housekeeper answered. "Tis you again, Cillian O'Cleary!" she said with a queer tone and a sly look. He was taken aback slightly, then hesitantly said, "Hello Mrs. Murray. We're here to put up the fence."

"Aye, you are indeed. Around back. Mr. Murray is waiting."

They set up their tools and worked through the afternoon. Near sundown, they quit for the day. The day worker would return in the morning, and Cillian set up a lean-to in the wooded area behind the house. Mr Murray gave him some food and drink for the night.

As he was about to walk back to his lean-to, he caught sight of the young lady of the house. She was sixteen and lovely, wearing a white chemise dress. She had long, shiny auburn hair. She looked directly at him, and their eyes locked. They were both stunned, and it seemed as if the orange glow of sunset flickered around them. She smiled. He was stunned but managed a nervous smile. She hurried away.

They finished the installation the next day. Cillian settled up with Mr. Murray and the day worker. He packed his tools and made his way back down Main Street. On his way down the slope to the ferryman a teen aged girl slipped out from behind some thick bushes and stopped Cillian. He was surprised to see one of the girls who worked in the house with Mrs. Murray. She was wearing a hood and cloak over her dress. She put her shush finger to her lips and handed him a note then ran up the slope.

Cillian opened the note. It was written in script on fine paper.

'Cillian, you are invited to a midnight Rendezvous in the wood behind Lady Swetereyun's House, but further back near the river's edge, in two-week's time on Saturday the 18th. Cider and dancing under a full moon! Do not tell a soul, for it is a private occasion.' He tucked the note in his tool pouch.

He got home late, so the next morning he would ask his brothers' advice, but when they were getting ready for work, he couldn't say anything about the note.

He'd only had brief encounters with girls and didn't know much—girls who wanted to be married at fourteen. But Finn had experience. As to what extent, Cillian didn't know. Gentleman keep quiet about such things.

He was going to ask the blacksmith for advice, but he thought better since it concerned a customer. And when he thought about it that way, he tried to forget the invitation, except it was all he could think about. He kept seeing the young lady, Sweteryun smiling at him. And the brave girl with the sly look in her eye handing him the note.

In a few days, he started to dream about Sweteryun. Nothing obscene or lascivious.

Just wistful, quick dreams in dark places but not nightmarish.

On the night of the seventeenth, he dreamt he and Sweteryun were running barefoot on the lawn of a large estate. They were dressed in fine clothing. It was twilight, and there was a low hum in his ears.

Ahead was a great Manor House. They went up the stairs on the south veranda and into a darkened ballroom. They joined a slow Waltz. He didn't know he could dance. They turned about the room a few times to the music of a chamber orchestra.

Suddenly he stood before a man in a black gentleman's coat with a slightly ruffled white shirt buttoned to the neck. He could not see his face. He awoke with a start and was sweating profusely.

The next day was the 18th. Full moon. He hurried home and cleaned up. Burning with anticipation, he set out at 10:30.

It was a warm summer night in July, a was mostly dry month, and the clouds were sparse. The night insects were in full chorus, but Cillian didn't hear them. He walked for about twenty minutes and reached the shallow river that encircled High Bluff. He borrowed a row boat along the banks and rowed quietly over the calm water.

On Main Street, a few revellers were milling outside a pub, but he ducked away from them. When he arrived at Seweryn's, he silently went behind the wooded area and found a well-worn path. It led to a clearing near a bluff. He walked into the clearing, and the moonlight shone on him as if it were almost daylight.

Three maidens appeared from nearby bushes giggling. Two were fourteen, one was sixteen. Cillian recognised the one who handed him the note. She whispered, "You know me. I'm Comfort. This is Hitty. Have some cider, it's just two weeks old." He drank and didn't know what to say. "Let's dance," Hitty said as Cillian finished his small drink. Sweteryun looked on.

He was embarrassed a little. He didn't know any dances but the girls danced around him and sang together in almost whispers a popular love ballad that he'd heard somewhere recently. He was getting a little light headed and was beginning to be taken in by their wiles when Sweteryun touched his arm.

He turned around. She was smiling. 'Sweteryun', he said. She was beautiful in a summer dress and her auburn hair fell about her shoulders.

They chatted for a while, Cillians' mild jitters eased by the fermented cider.

Then abruptly Cillian held Sweteryun in the waltz stance. She was surprised, but she followed his lead as the others hummed a popular waltz tune. They swung around the clearing and he said to her, "We danced in a ballroom last night, in a dream. Do you remember?" She just smiled.

After a few minutes she pulled away but held onto his hand and she ran lightly with him across the clearing and down a path that led to a bluff overlooking the shallow river. They sat near the edge on soft grass. She started asking him questions about himself and his family and all at once he was glib and could talk easily with her, as if they had known each other for some time They spoke for what seemed hours. She asked him what his name meant. "Church", he said. He asked her hers "sweet and mysterious," she replied. Both of them were shining in the moonlight.

It was nearly three am. It was warm and still. The riotous insects fell silent around them. Even across the river, they were quiet. The two girls, lurking a few yards back on the path spying, suddenly felt a powerful presence near them and crouched in the bushes as it passed.

Cillian and Sweteryun were quiet, too. Looking into each other's eyes, their heart's welled up. They kissed softly, then passionately, embracing. Just then, The Nightmare emerged from the path and crouched near them, wild-eyed with riotous hair and dressed in an ill-fitting dirty nightgown. The two hadn't noticed. They had lain back on the grass and were kissing. The Nightmare took hold of Sweteryun gently. She encouraged her to lift her head and to cascade her hair about him. She kissed him again while The Nightmare cast a binding spell on Cillian that could never be broken until the deed was done.

The two girls were rising from the bushes when they heard footsteps and then a low voice which they recognised and sent terror through them. "You two. Stay where you are," Mrs Murray said in a whispering command as she rushed by them.

Cillian and Sweteryun were still embracing when Mrs Murray entered the clearing at the bluff. The Nightmare turned her head and stared at her with bulging eyes and a crazy grin. "Shoo Cailleach," she said and waved her hand. The Nightmare flew off, and the two lovers jumped to their feet.

There was a moment of sad silence as Mrs Murray looked at the Love Light radiating from them, her grim demeanour softening some. Then she said, harshly, "Sweteryun, come with me girl. You, Cillian O'Cleary, I don't care if your mother was a Mondragon. If you ever mention this to anyone I will have Mr. Murray beat you to within an inch of your life. And your brother too."

"Yes ma'am," he replied. Sweteryun turned to him, still glowing in the moonlight, and said sadly, "Goodbye Cillian."

There was finality in her tone. He stood stock still, watching her walk away.

The three girls and the woman walked the path in silence until they had nearly reached the house. Mrs Murray stopped abruptly. Whispering, she said, "The three of you have made a mess that could be construed as a scandal and that, Swetheryun, could turn you into a spinster. The three of you seen as trollops. This won't do. I'm sending you a week earlier to Boston to your mother while she arranges your marriage. God forbid your father hears of this while he's away. He'd send the sheriff after that boy. And you two are going back to your mothers." All three were crying. Still whispering, she said, "A bit of advice. The Cailleach is not to be trifled with," as they began to plead their innocence Mrs Murray made the 'shh' sign and motioned them to follow her, creeping toward the house so as not to wake Mr Murray.

Cillian made his way home and crept into his house as quietly as he could. It was almost sun rise. He didn't sleep much. He was lovesick. *It will pass*, he thought.

But it didn't. The days were filled with work, but when he lay on his bed to sleep, the night with Swetheryun played repeatedly. It rankled his heart with bittersweet resentment. He'd kissed other girls. What was it? He understood that he could never marry a girl like her, poor as he was, so he would forget her. But he couldn't.

Everyone who knew him could tell something was wrong. He didn't talk much with anyone except his brother and the blacksmith. As warned, he did not tell anyone of that moonlit night.

One evening he had a hankering to look through his parents' things that he and Finn had kept on a shelf. It was in a corner above a table where his mother had taught them to read. Among the items that gave him sad nostalgia, he found the O'Cleary and Mondragon Family Crests on plaques that were propped up against the wall. His father's was for knights, but his mother's was a bit different. The knight's helmet at the top was self-explanatory but the two fire-breathing dragons holding a disembodied hand meant magic powers for the knight in all his endeavours, and the red X at the bottom meant unseen forces helping the Knight.

Apparently, the Mondragon clan were mercenaries but only for established and trusted allies. That night he dreamt of being a soldier.

As promised weeks before, Mrs Murray sent Swetheryun to Boston along with a sealed letter. It was for Mrs Barry only.

When Swetheryun arrived too soon at the fine townhouse Mr Barry had secured in the North End, Mrs. Barry knew something was awry. Mr Murray handed her the letter and she sat in a window seat to read it. "Dear Mrs

Barry," it began. "There is no cause for undue alarm, but I am compelled to inform you the following; the new fence had been installed by a strapping and handsome young man by the name of Cillian O'Cleary. The three girls, unbeknownst to me, arranged for a moonlit rendezvous out in the back wood a few nights ago. Something woke me with a start, and I hurried there on a hunch and found them. Though innocent it was, the Cailleach was hovering over Swetheryun and the young man. I don't have to tell you, of all people, what this could mean, but, Cill is old Irish for Church and O'Cleary clergy. His mother was a Mondragon. I threatened him to keep his mouth shut. Mr Murray will look into that when he returns. Please forgive my dullard senses for not seeing this before it happened. Something befuddled me."

Mrs Barry folded the letter and put it in a secret compartment within her travel chest.

She paced back and forth for a while, thinking about the situation. She had a hunch but now realised why Sweteryun's pretty green eyes were so dreamy. She looked forlornly into the wall mirror and said, "I'll take care of it", in a sad voice.

When he was about to return to New Jersey, Mr Murray was quietly instructed to visit the young blacksmith. She muttered a sentence. He nodded in understanding and left.

It had been six weeks since that unfortunate night. Cillian lay awake, resisting the temptation to run to Swetheryun. The thought of her wiles, laughter, glib conversation, and kisses whirled in his mind. The blacksmith had hollered at him so many times he'd gotten a bit horse.

There was vague talk about young love, and Cillian had something to do with it. The blacksmith thought Cillian was possibly smitten by one of the girls from the house in High Bluff. He'd hoped the customer hadn't been roiled by it.

Cillian was in the back of the blacksmith's shop unloading smelted bar iron from Batsto Village. He finished, and as he rounded the front of the shop, there stood Mr Murray and the blacksmith talking. Almost on cue, Mr Murray said, "Oh, and the Barry's girl, Sweteryun, she's betrothed to a fine young man from a well-connected family in Boston. They'll be married in a few months." Cillian felt as if he'd been felled by a tree. His heart sank in his chest. He entered the shop and hid in a corner, his mind racing. The blacksmith had seen the reaction to the news, and he immediately knew what had happened. Mr Murray gave the blacksmith a sidelong glance and bid him good day.

"Cillian, what happened?" the blacksmith, a dark-haired hulking man, was worried about gossip. He had worked hard to build his business. He also empathetically saw the young man's turmoil. "Nothing she'd be ashamed of," he croaked, "That's all I can say. I trust you to keep it to yourself. I haven't even told my brother. I'm done unloading. Can I leave?" "Go on. On the morrow," replied the perturbed blacksmith.

The next day Cillian did not show up for work. He left only a note for his brother asking him to thank the blacksmith and that he was off to join the new Marine Corps. Both his brother and the blacksmith were stunned. His bother guessed it was a girl. He had heard something too. Cillian said he'd return when he could.

After training camp, Cillian was deployed to the Barbary Coast, where he encountered and fought Saracens to the death with swords and scabbards. Eventually he was given a detail, with seven other Marines and two Navy midshipmen, to aid William Eaton in crossing the North African Desert. It was the first US covert operation and laid the groundwork to end the Barbary Pirates. He was shot at the Battle of Derne.

He died for several minutes from a wound to the chest. The shot was removed, and he recovered, but like other people who have died and come back to life, he could see and converse with ghosts. For the rest of his enlistment, he was known as the ghost talker, as he was seen on many occasions having a conversation with thin air. The brass heard about it and brought him in for special training. He was honourably discharged when his hitch was up. He then joined the reserves and made himself available for other duties.

It was eight years later, and Cillian had finally made it back home. His brother had gotten married and had children. Finn had his own schooner and was building a business. Cillian spent some time with them, but he wanted to travel south. He did, but only as far as West Jersey, now South Jersey. He had stopped in a town called Batsto to work for a while in an iron foundry. A few weeks passed, and the town's blacksmith and helper died when the blacksmith's building collapsed. The furnace was largely untouched, and Cillian couldn't pass up the opportunity.

Soon after he rebuilt the shop, he became very busy and had to hire two helpers. He was liked by most of the people in the area, but some of the people were suspicious. A soldier with a battle scar on his left cheek shows up, then the blacksmith's building falls on him, and Cillian moves in.

There were several widows around and very young girls who would flirt with him all over town, but a Lenapi girl caught his eye. They married and were shunned by the settlers and the Lenape.

He built a spacious log cabin with many rooms on a bank of the Mullica River. There they lived for decades but could not have children. The Medicine Woman said the Great Kitanitowit would not allow it. She didn't know why. Other settlers and Lenapi had children. She said it was something to do with Cillians' future.

Then one morning, Cillians wife didn't wake up. She died in her sleep. Cillians grief grew into anger. He noticed he'd grown angry while enlisted. He found it easy to get enraged and fight and kill. A fortune teller in Tripoli said he'd had the spell of the broken hearted.

Unrequited love. His wife said the same thing, but he denied it. She had made him happy. At the same time, he hadn't realised how close he had gotten to her, and the grief was horrible. He was getting angry again.

When he was leaving the Marine Corp., he was asked by his lieutenant (Cillian was a sergeant) if he would make himself available for special duty should the need arise. Cillian agreed, and about six months after his wife died, a man in black clothes and a cloak breezed in the side door of his blacksmith's shop. Cillian knew immediately that the man was dead.

Well, dead in one level of awareness but quite alive in another. How exactly it worked, Cillian hadn't the faintest, but he accepted it, remembering how he'd died and seen another world of beauty but was dragged back.

"Marine," the man began as he produced credentials, "Rotgut". "Oasis," Cillian replied. An entertaining Code that was popular back in the day. He, his lieutenant and the entourage had to drink fetid water from a dying oasis. That got around the Corp. "My condolences on your wife's passing. My name is Smythe." After some shop talk about Cillian's' trade Smythe said, "There is some pressing business that needs to be addressed. It's to do with witchcraft."

Cillian had heard a war story about entire legions of Roman soldiers that couldn't sleep from night terrors during the first Roman invasion of Britain. Not long after the invasion Caeser marched the Legions out of Britain and sailed to Gaul.

Druids.

"Not too keen on fighting witches," Cillian replied.

"You won't be fighting an air war. We must quietly remove several organisers who are beginning heinous human sacrifices, especially on children, to satisfy their evil demons and gain power. This is how severe corruption begins. There are a few groups in New Jersey, Philadelphia, Connecticut, and New York. I will give you names and addresses. I will be near every target and point them out to you. And, by the way, we needed you in this vicinity, so we arranged for the shop to fall on the other blacksmith and his helper. It turns out the two of them were responsible for the disappearance of a young woman. Do you want to hear the rest?"

"No," Cillian replied.

And so it began. He underwent bizarre overnight sweating in bed and lung ailments for months before his first mission. Smythe told him it would help to make him invisible or at least unnoticed. And an occasional shocking discomfort down his left leg—spells from unseen good witches. He suffered it.

He was well-trained and had killed a number of men in battles and skirmishes so he had no problem killing monsters. His first target he simply through off a bridge into swollen river-not many people knew how to swim in those days. The second was a politician he launched down a staircase in Independence Hall, Philadelphia, head first. There were several others over a two-month period which required other means of assassination, and word had gotten around in those evil circles that a phantom was collecting, so they thought.

Sacrifices ceased. But Smythes' strategy was to wait for a spell.

Meanwhile a few people in Batsto were noticing that Cillian was absent days at a time and news of the Pennsylvania politicians' mysterious death was big news. His cover was specialty supply runs, and he did bring items back with him but he decided it was time to move. He sold his shop to his helper but kept his log cabin for summer use. He told everyone he was moving back to Paulus Hook, just recently named Jersey City, to be near his brother and sister in law.

He did go to his family for a while but then he set off to wander about the region. Some of the old colonies became his territory. He'd worked as a blacksmith but he really rid the world of human offal along with Smythe. Interestingly, the more he executed, the more invisible he became until he was, for the most part, living with people who had been brought back from spirit to a physical world unseen by most.

Although he reached middle age he outlived his brother and sister in law. But he stepped away as his nephews and nieces got old because he knew he would out live them too. He'd become a warlock, a man who could step between worlds. He'd live for hundreds of years but always looked like he was in his 50s or thereabouts.

As the Industrial Age moved into mechanisation concerning blacksmithing, he picked up woodworking and kept busy with his executioners job, which waxed and waned. The Eye was always watching.

Around 1900, he had a very strange dream that he couldn't forget. He was riding in a large bus, more modern than the ones he knew, on a ramp along the Hudson River.

It was a bright sunny day, clear as a bell. He was stunned to see the NYC skyline across the river, including two incredible new towers downtown. The bus then started heading toward tunnel openings, but what caught his eye was a giant billboard along the ramp with a handsome young man wearing a fashionable suit jacket and tie with a full head of rustic hair in a style he hadn't seen since the 1790s. 'Don Mulqueen-Mens Apparel' under the giant picture.

When he awoke, he realised the face on the billboard was his. He chuckled and said to the wall, 'Very funny'.

He was busy taking care of 'business' during much of the 20th century.

But the population had grown substantially, and in the 1950s, a rocket propulsion engineer and his occult followers managed to break open the veil between the physical and the spirit worlds in Los Angeles that unleashed vile parasitic spirits. Not long after, an immigration explosion and satanic ritual abuse organisations sprung up nationwide. It was overwhelming—a mess by the 2020s.

Smythe informed him that there would be a dimensional shift for allied families to a new level of the world. "Too crowded here, and too many predators," Smythe had said. Cillian was needed in the new world and he would have more opportunities to move up.

One day in late September of 2022, Cillian had gone into lower Manhattan to hand deliver a file to an operator who lived in the Bowery—a favour for Smythe, who said he was very busy.

After making the drop, he thought he'd get a cup of coffee. On the way to the subway, he spied The Coffee Klotch.

He walked in and up to the counter. Behind the counter, two young women were busy tidying up workspaces and making coffee. One of them was tuning the radio dial. Another young woman was at the counter glancing at a notebook that was propped up-it said Julliard on the cover. She looked up. The radio stopped crackling and a song was playing… 'Should we lose each other in the shadow of the evening trees I'll wait for you, should I fall behind wait for me', went the lyrics.

"Can I help you sir?" As their eyes met, there was a shock of recognition. Cillian instantly knew she was Sweteryun, though obviously now someone else; he could see a resemblance, especially around her eyes.

She, too, had a strange sensation when she saw him but went about filling his order. "Have you been to Hoboken? I thought I recognised you from that Coffee Klotch" Cillian fibbed. "Only a couple of times for orientation," she replied and as she looked up at him, their eyes locked, and a memory of dancing barefoot in the moonlight flashed through her mind. She stood up straight, taking a breath in astonishment. She was about to speak when a tall, handsome, lanky young man busted through the front door. "Gabba gabba hey," he said. Ruby, who was Swetheryun, giggled. Cillians' left leg shocked a little.

In an epiphany, Cillian saw the big picture. This was Sweteryun's husband from Boston. Cillian knew them from hundreds of years ago, and probably more. Cillian understood that he and Sweteryun had met when they were young and played their respective parts in the Mysteries at that time. Cillian had a job to do. She looked back at Cillian and smiled with recognition. He saw that in her eyes and smiled. He and Alton nodded to each other as he walked out.

He realised that he had lost any emotional attachment to Sweteryun a long time ago, even though the memories of that night were just as vivid as they were over two hundred years ago. It was closure, but he knew he'd see her again in the Alternate world.

Cillian thought he'd take a bus instead of the train and wandered over to Eighth Avenue. He was still thrilled about seeing Sweteryun. He was wondering if she had gone into the service. He turned a corner onto Eighth and was absolutely stunned by a four hundred foot 3D painting of Sweteryun as a lovely witch under an umbrella. Just then, a plumber's van stopped in traffic. A man leaned out the window, looked directly at Cillian and, pointing up at the ad, said, "Dat I would marry!"

The van rolled on, and Cillian broke into convulsive, silent laughter as a weight lifted from his heart.